THE DOUBLE CLUE

AND

OTHER HERCULE POIROT STORIES

HERCULE POIROT ALSO APPEARS IN

The Mysterious Affair at Styles
The Murder on the Links
Poirot Investigates
The Murder of Roger Ackroyd
The Big Four
The Mystery of the Blue Train
Peril at End House
Lord Edgware Dies
Murder on the Orient Express
Three Act Tragedy
Death in the Clouds
The ABC Murders
Murder in Mesopotamia
Cards on the Table
Murder in the Mews
Dumb Witness
Death on the Nile
Appointment With Death
Hercule Poirot's Christmas

AND MANY MORE

Agatha Christie®

The Double Clue

AND
OTHER HERCULE POIROT STORIES

Selected and introduced by
Sophie Hannah and John Curran

HARPER

HARPER

An imprint of HarperCollins*Publishers*
1 London Bridge Street
London SE1 9GF
www.harpercollins.co.uk

Published by Harper for Quick Reads 2016

'The Disappearance of Mr Davenheim' and 'The Adventure of the Egyptian Tomb' first published in the UK in *Poirot Investigates* 1924
'The Double Clue' and 'The Market Basing Mystery'
first published in the UK in *Poirot's Early Cases* 1974

Some words and phrases in this book have been edited
to fulfil the aims of the Quick Reads project.

Agatha Christie® Poirot®
Copyright © 1924, 1974 by Agatha Christie Limited. All rights reserved.
www.agathachristie.com

A catalogue record for this book is
available from the British Library

ISBN 978-0-00-816509-3

Set in ITC Stone Serif by Born Group using Atomik ePublisher from Easypress

Printed and bound in Great Britain by
Clays Ltd, St Ives plc

MIX
Paper from
responsible sources
FSC **FSC® C007454**
www.fsc.org

FSC is a non-profit international organisation established to promote
the responsible management of the world's forests. Products carrying the
FSC label are independently certified to assure consumers that they come
from forests that are managed to meet the social, economic and
ecological needs of present and future generations,
and other controlled sources.

Find out more about HarperCollins and the environment at
www.harpercollins.co.uk/green

Contents

Introduction

Agatha Christie is the bestselling novelist of all time. Only the Bible and Shakespeare have sold more copies than her books. Readers all over the world have adored her stories for decades. So what makes her work so incredibly popular, and why is she still worth reading today?

I think the answers to these questions have something to do with the way that Agatha Christie manages to blend opposites in a seamless and perfect way. Her books are so simple that they can be enjoyed by children, yet at the same time the puzzles within them are complex challenges for the bright adult mind.

Her detective Hercule Poirot is a strange mixture of opposites too: his powers of observation, his grasp of logic, his intelligence, his understanding of the human mind – these are all superhuman traits, but he is also very much an ordinary human being, with his fussy, annoying habits and his obsession with his moustache. We take him very seriously, yet we also laugh fondly at him. We love him, though he sometimes infuriates us. He clearly has great depth and is wise and experienced, yet we never learn any details of his past.

Agatha Christie's mysteries always grapple with questions of good and evil, and she shows time and time again that she is fully aware of the darkness that lingers inside us all. Yet – again, in a seamless blend of apparent opposites – her novels and short stories are not depressing or bleak to read. Rather, her tales are huge fun and have plenty of the feel-good factor.

Above all, Agatha Christie is a genius storyteller. She understood that readers want a great story more than they want anything else. And time and time again, over a career that spanned many decades, great stories were what she gave us. Hooray for Agatha Christie!

Sophie Hannah

1

The Market Basing Mystery is the perfect introduction to Agatha's work if you've never read her stories before. Everything she does best is done in this story: it is a very short but perfect showcase of her talents as a mystery writer. This is the hundred-metre sprint of Poirot stories, ideal for those readers who want to witness Agatha's greatness in the shortest possible time! The narrator, the 'I' character, is Poirot's friend and helper, Captain Arthur Hastings.

Sophie Hannah

The Market Basing Mystery

'After all, there's nothing like the country, is there?' said Inspector Japp, breathing in heavily through his nose and out through his mouth in the most approved fashion.

Poirot and I agreed heartily. It had been the Scotland Yard inspector's idea that we should all go for the weekend to the little country town of Market Basing. When off duty, Japp was an ardent botanist, and spoke about tiny flowers with lengthy Latin names (somewhat strangely pronounced) with even more enthusiasm than he gave to his cases.

'Nobody knows us, and we know nobody,' explained Japp. 'That's the idea.'

This was not to prove quite the case, however, for the local police constable happened to have been transferred from a village fifteen miles away where a case of arsenic poisoning had brought him into contact with the Scotland Yard man.

However, his delight on recognising the great man only enhanced Japp's sense of well-being. As we sat down to breakfast on Sunday morning in the parlour of the village inn, with the sun shining, and honeysuckle thrusting in at the window, we were all in the best of spirits. The bacon and eggs were excellent, the coffee not so good, but passable and boiling hot.

'This is the life,' said Japp. 'When I retire, I shall have a little place in the country. Far from crime, like this!'

'Crime is everywhere,' said Poirot, helping himself to a neat square of bread, and frowning at a sparrow which had balanced itself impertinently on the windowsill.

I quoted lightly:

'That rabbit has a pleasant face,
His private life is a disgrace
I really could not tell to you
The awful things that rabbits do.'

'Lord,' said Japp, stretching himself backwards, 'I believe I could manage another egg, and perhaps a rasher or two of bacon. What do you say, Captain?'

'I'm with you,' I replied heartily. 'What about you, Poirot?'

Poirot shook his head.

'One must not fill the stomach so much that the brain refuses to function,' he remarked.

'I'll risk filling the stomach a bit more,' laughed Japp. 'I take a large size in stomachs; and by the way, you're getting stout yourself, Monsieur Poirot. Here, miss, eggs and bacon twice.'

At that moment, however, an imposing form blocked the doorway. It was Constable Pollard.

'I hope you'll excuse me troubling the inspector, gentlemen, but I'd be glad of his advice.'

'I'm on holiday,' said Japp hastily. 'No work for me. What is the case?'

'Gentleman up at Leigh House – shot himself – through the head.'

'Well, they will do it,' said Japp in a matter-of-fact way. 'Debt, or a woman, I suppose. Sorry I can't help you, Pollard.'

'The point is,' said the constable, 'that he can't have shot himself. Leastways, that's what Dr Giles says.'

Japp put down his cup.

'*Can't* have shot himself? What do you mean?'

'That's what Dr Giles says,' repeated Pollard. 'He says it's quite impossible. He's puzzled to death, the door being locked on the inside and the windows bolted; but he sticks to it that the man couldn't have committed suicide.'

That settled it. The further supply of bacon and eggs was waved aside, and a few minutes later we were all walking as fast as we could in the direction of Leigh House, with Japp eagerly questioning the constable.

The name of the deceased was Walter Protheroe; he was a man of middle age and something of a recluse. He had come to Market Basing eight years ago and rented Leigh House, a rambling old mansion fast falling into ruin. He lived in a corner of it, his wants attended to by a housekeeper whom he had brought with him. Miss Clegg was her name, and she was a very superior woman and highly thought of in the village.

Just lately Mr Protheroe had had visitors staying with him, a Mr and Mrs Parker from London. This morning, unable to get a reply when she went to call her employer, and finding the door locked, Miss Clegg became alarmed, and telephoned for the police and the doctor. Constable Pollard and Dr Giles had arrived at the same moment. Together they had broken down the oak door of his bedroom.

Mr Protheroe was lying on the floor, shot through the head, and the pistol was clasped in his right hand. It looked a clear case of suicide.

After examining the body, however, Dr Giles became very puzzled, and finally drew the constable aside, and explained his confusion; whereupon Pollard had at once thought of Japp. Leaving the doctor in charge, he had hurried down to the inn.

By the time the constable's tale was over, we had arrived at Leigh House, a big, desolate house surrounded by an unkempt, weed-ridden garden. The front door was open, and we passed at once into the hall. We heard voices coming from a small morning room so we entered it. Four people were in the room: a somewhat flashily dressed man with a shifty, unpleasant face to whom I took an immediate dislike; a woman of much the same type, though handsome in a coarse fashion; another woman dressed in neat black who stood apart from the rest, and whom I took to be the housekeeper; and a tall man dressed in sporting tweeds, with a clever, capable face, and who was clearly in command of the situation.

'Dr Giles,' said the constable, 'this is Detective-Inspector Japp of Scotland Yard, and his two friends.'

The doctor greeted us and introduced us to Mr and Mrs Parker. Then we went upstairs. At a sign from Japp, Pollard remained below, as it were on guard over the household. The doctor led us upstairs and along a passage. A door was open at the end; splinters hung from the hinges, and the door itself had crashed to the floor inside the room.

We went in. The body was still lying on the floor. Mr Protheroe had been a man of middle age, bearded, with hair grey at the temples. Japp went and knelt by the body.

'Why couldn't you leave it as you found it?' he grumbled.

The doctor shrugged his shoulders.

'We thought it a clear case of suicide.'

'H'm!' said Japp. 'Bullet entered the head behind the left ear.'

'Exactly,' said the doctor. 'Clearly impossible for him to have fired it himself. He'd have had to twist his hand right round his head. It couldn't have been done.'

'Yet you found the pistol clasped in his hand? Where is it, by the way?'

The doctor nodded to the table.

'But it wasn't clasped in his hand,' he said. 'It was inside the hand, but the fingers weren't closed over it.'

'Put there afterwards,' said Japp; 'that's clear enough.' He was examining the weapon. 'One cartridge fired. We'll test it for fingerprints, but I doubt if we'll find any but yours, Dr Giles. How long has he been dead?'

'Some time last night. I can't give the time to an hour or so, as those wonderful doctors in detective stories do. Roughly, he's been dead about twelve hours.'

So far, Poirot had not made a move of any kind. He had remained by my side, watching Japp at work and listening to his questions. Only, from time to time, he had sniffed the air very delicately, and as if puzzled. I too had sniffed, but could detect nothing of interest. The air seemed perfectly fresh and devoid of odour. And yet, from time to time, Poirot continued to sniff it dubiously, as though his keener nose detected something I had missed.

Now, as Japp moved away from the body, Poirot knelt down by it. He took no interest in the wound. I thought at first that he was examining the fingers of the hand that had held the pistol, but in a minute I saw that it was a handkerchief carried in the coat sleeve that interested him. Mr Protheroe was dressed in a dark grey lounge suit. Finally Poirot got up from his knees, but his eyes still strayed back to the handkerchief as though puzzled.

Japp called to him to come and help to lift the door. Seizing my opportunity, I too knelt down, and taking the handkerchief from the sleeve, studied it minutely. It was a perfectly plain handkerchief of white cambric; there was no mark or stain on it of any kind. I replaced it, shaking my head. I was baffled.

The others had raised the door. I realized that they were hunting for the key. They looked in vain.

'That settles it,' said Japp. 'The window's shut and bolted. The murderer left by the door, locking it and taking the key with him. He thought it would be accepted that Protheroe had locked himself in and shot himself, and that the absence of the key would not be noticed. You agree, Monsieur Poirot?'

'I agree, yes; but it would have been simpler and better to slip the key back inside the room under the door. Then it would look as though it had fallen from the lock.'

'Ah, well, you can't expect everybody to have the bright ideas that you have. You'd have been a holy terror if you'd taken to crime. Any remarks to make, Monsieur Poirot?'

Poirot, it seemed to me, was somewhat at a loss. He looked round the room and remarked mildly: 'He smoked a lot, this monsieur.'

True enough, the grate was filled with cigarette-stubs, as was an ashtray that stood on a small table near the big armchair.

'He must have got through about twenty cigarettes last night,' remarked Japp. Stooping down, he examined the contents of the grate carefully, then looked at the ashtray. 'They're all the same kind,' he announced, 'and smoked by the same man. There's nothing there, Monsieur Poirot.'

'I did not suggest that there was,' murmured my friend.

'Ha,' cried Japp, 'what's this?' He pounced on something bright and glittering that lay on the floor near the dead man. 'A broken cufflink. I wonder who this belongs to. Dr Giles, would you please go down and send up the housekeeper.'

'What about the Parkers? He's very anxious to leave the house – says he's got urgent business in London.'

'I dare say. It'll have to get on without him. By the way things are going, it's likely that there'll be some urgent business down here for him to attend to! Send up the housekeeper, and don't let either of the Parkers give you and Pollard the slip. Did any of the household come in here this morning?'

The doctor reflected.

'No, they stood outside in the corridor while Pollard and I came in.'

'Sure of that?'

'Absolutely certain.'

The doctor went off on his mission.

'Good man, that,' said Japp. 'Some of these sporting doctors are first-class fellows. Well, I wonder who shot this chap. It looks like one

11

of the three in the house. I hardly suspect the housekeeper. She's had eight years to shoot him if she wanted to. I wonder who these Parkers are? They're not a very attractive couple.'

At this moment the housekeeper, Miss Clegg, appeared. She was a thin, gaunt woman with neat grey hair parted in the middle, very staid and calm in manner. However, there was an air of efficiency about her which commanded respect. In answer to Japp's questions, she explained that she had worked for the dead man for fourteen years. He had been a generous and considerate employer.

She had never seen Mr and Mrs Parker until three days ago, when they arrived unexpectedly to stay. She guessed that they had asked themselves – Mr Protheroe had certainly not seemed pleased to see them. The cufflinks which Japp showed her had not belonged to Mr Protheroe – she was sure of that. Questioned about the pistol, she said that she believed her employer had a weapon of that kind. He kept it locked up. She had seen it once some years ago, but could not say whether this was the same one.

She had heard no shot last night, but that was not surprising, as it was a big, rambling house, and her rooms and those prepared for the Parkers were at the other end of the building. She did not know what time Mr Protheroe had gone to bed – he was still up when she retired at half past nine. It was not his habit to go at once to bed when he went to his room. Usually he would sit up half the night, reading and smoking. He was a great smoker.

Then Poirot added a question of his own:

'Did Mr Protheroe sleep with his window open or shut, as a rule?'

Miss Clegg considered.

'It was usually open, at any rate at the top.'

'Yet now it is closed. Can you explain that?'

'No, unless he felt a draught and shut it.'

Japp asked her a few more questions and then dismissed her. Next he interviewed the Parkers separately. Mrs Parker was upset and tearful; Mr Parker was full of bluster and abuse. He denied that the cufflink was his, yet his wife had previously recognized it, and as he had also denied ever having been in Protheroe's room, Japp reckoned that he had enough evidence to apply for a warrant for Parker's arrest.

Leaving Pollard in charge, Japp bustled back to the village and phoned headquarters. Poirot and I strolled back to the inn.

'You're unusually quiet,' I said. 'Doesn't the case interest you?'

'Oh yes! It interests me enormously. But it puzzles me also.'

'The motive is obscure,' I said, 'but I'm certain that Parker's a bad lot. The case against him seems pretty clear but for the lack of motive, and that may come out later.'

'Nothing struck you as being significant, although overlooked by Japp?'

I looked at him curiously.

'What have you got up your sleeve, Poirot?'

'What did the dead man have up his sleeve?'

'Oh, that handkerchief!'

'Exactly, that handkerchief.'

'A sailor carries his handkerchief in his sleeve,' I said thoughtfully.

'An excellent point, Hastings, though not the one I had in mind.'

'Anything else?'

'Yes, over and over again I go back to the smell of cigarette smoke.'

'I didn't smell any,' I said in surprise.

'No more did I, my dear friend.'

I looked earnestly at him. It is so difficult to know when Poirot is teasing, but he seemed serious and was frowning to himself.

The inquest took place two days later. In the meantime other evidence emerged. A tramp had admitted that he had climbed over the wall into the Leigh House garden, where he often slept in a shed that was left unlocked. He declared that at twelve o'clock he had heard two men quarrelling loudly in a room on the first floor. One was demanding a sum of money; the other was angrily refusing. Concealed behind a bush, he had seen the two men as they passed and repassed the lighted window. One he knew well to be Mr Protheroe, the owner of the house; the other he identified positively as Mr Parker.

It was clear now that the Parkers had come to Leigh House to blackmail Protheroe. Later it was discovered that the dead man's real name was Wendover. He had been a lieutenant in the Navy and had been concerned in the blowing up of the first-class cruiser *Merrythought* in 1910. The case seemed to be becoming clear. It was supposed that Parker knew of the part Wendover had played, had tracked him down and demanded hush-money which the other refused to pay. In the course of the quarrel, Wendover drew his revolver. Parker snatched it from him and shot him. Then he tried to make the murder look like suicide.

At the police court Parker was committed for trial, reserving his defence. As we left, Poirot nodded his head.

'It must be so,' he murmured to himself. 'Yes, it must be so. I will delay no longer.'

He went into the post office, and wrote a note which he sent by special messenger. I did not see to whom it was addressed. Then we returned to the inn where we had stayed on that memorable weekend.

Poirot was restless, going to and from the window.

'I await a visitor,' he explained. 'It cannot be – surely it cannot be that I am mistaken? No, here she is.'

To my utter astonishment, a minute later Miss Clegg walked into the room. She was less calm than usual, and was breathing hard as though she had been running. I saw the fear in her eyes as she looked at Poirot.

'Sit down, miss,' he said kindly. 'I guessed rightly, did I not?'

Her answer was to burst into tears.

'Why did you do it?' asked Poirot gently. 'Why?'

'I loved him so,' she answered. 'I was nursemaid to him when he was a little boy. Oh, be merciful to me!'

'I will do all I can. But you understand that I cannot permit an innocent man to hang – even though he is an unpleasant scoundrel.'

She sat up and said in a low voice: 'Perhaps in the end I could not have, either. Do whatever must be done.'

Then, rising, she hurried from the room.

'Did she shoot him?' I asked utterly bewildered.

Poirot smiled and shook his head.

'He shot himself. Do you remember that he carried his handkerchief in his *right* sleeve? That showed me that he was left-handed. Fearing exposure, after his stormy interview with Mr Parker, he shot himself. In the morning Miss Clegg came to call him as usual and found him lying dead. As she has just told us, she had known him since he was a little boy, and was furious with the Parkers, who had driven him to this shameful death. She saw them as murderers, and then suddenly she saw a chance of making them suffer for the deed they had inspired.

'She alone knew that he was left-handed. She changed the pistol to his right hand, closed and bolted the window and dropped the bit of cuff-link she had picked up in one of the downstairs rooms. Then she went out, locking the door and removing the key.'

'Poirot,' I said, in a burst of enthusiasm, 'you are magnificent. All that from the one little clue of the handkerchief.'

'And the cigarette smoke. If the window had been closed, and all those cigarettes smoked, the room ought to have been full of stale tobacco.

'Instead, it was perfectly fresh, so I deduced at once that the window must have been open all night, and only closed in the morning. That gave me a very interesting line of speculation. I could think of no reason for a murderer to want to shut the window. It would be to his advantage to leave it open, and pretend that the murderer had escaped that way, if the theory of suicide was rejected. Of course, the tramp's evidence, when I heard it, confirmed my suspicions. He could never have overheard that conversation unless the window had been open.'

'Splendid!' I said heartily. 'Now, what about some tea?'

'Spoken like a true Englishman,' said Poirot with a sigh. 'I suppose it is not likely that I could obtain here a glass of blackcurrant liqueur?'

2

The problem posed in *The Disappearance of Mr Davenheim* seems a simple one: what happened to the well-known banker Mr Davenheim, after he walked out of his house one Saturday afternoon – and disappeared? Poirot takes up a challenge to solve this mystery without ever leaving his own flat! For this case Poirot is literally an armchair detective. Hastings, Poirot's friend and assistant, thinks that the answer is obvious and offers a few theories but Poirot is more cautious. Although this story was written almost a hundred years ago, one part of Mr Davenheim's adventure will be very familiar to modern readers. The solution, like many in the stories of Agatha Christie, is very simple; but only if you are as smart as Hercule Poirot!

John Curran

The Disappearance of
Mr Davenheim

Poirot and I were expecting our old friend Inspector Japp of Scotland Yard to tea. We were sitting round the tea table waiting for him. Poirot had just finished arranging the cups and saucers which our landlady was in the habit of throwing, rather than placing, on the table.

He had also breathed heavily on the metal teapot, and polished it with a silk handkerchief. The kettle was on the boil, and a small enamel saucepan beside it contained some thick, sweet chocolate which was more to Poirot's taste than what he called 'your English poison'.

A loud knock came from below, and a few minutes afterwards Japp entered briskly.

'Hope I'm not late,' he said as he greeted us. 'To tell the truth, I was chatting to Miller, the man who's in charge of the Davenheim case.'

That caught my attention. For the last three days the papers had been full of the strange disappearance of Mr Davenheim, senior partner of Davenheim and Salmon, the well-known bankers. He had walked out of his house last Saturday, and hadn't been seen since. I looked forward to hearing some details from Japp.

'I should have thought,' I said, 'that it would be almost impossible for anyone to "disappear" nowadays.'

Poirot moved a plate of bread and butter an eighth of an inch, and said sharply:

'Be exact, my friend. What do you mean by "disappear"? Which class of disappearance are you thinking of?'

'Are disappearances classified and labelled, then?' I laughed.

Japp smiled also. Poirot frowned at both of us.

'But certainly they are! They fall into three categories: First, and most common, the voluntary disappearance. Second, the much abused "loss of memory" case – rare, but occasionally genuine. Third, murder, and a more or less successful disposal of the body. Do think all three are impossible nowadays?'

'Very nearly so, I should think. You might lose your own memory, but someone would be sure to recognize you – especially a well-known man like Davenheim. Then "bodies" can't be made to vanish into thin air. Sooner or later they turn up, concealed in lonely places, or in trunks. Murder will be found out. In the same way, a runaway clerk, or husband or wife, is bound to be found in these days of radio and telephones. They can be headed off from foreign countries; ports and railway stations are watched; and as for hiding in this country, their features and appearance will be known to everyone who reads a daily newspaper. Such people are up against civilization.'

'My friend,' said Poirot, 'you make one error. You do not allow for the fact that a man who has decided to hide another man – or himself – might be that rare item, a man of method. He might bring intelligence, talent and a careful calculation of detail to the task; and then I do not see why he should not be able to baffle the police force.'

'But not *you*, I suppose?' said Japp good-humouredly, winking at me. 'He couldn't baffle you, eh, Monsieur Poirot?'

Poirot tried, and failed, to look modest.

'Me also! Why not? It is true that I approach such problems with an exact science, a mathematical precision, which seems, alas, only too rare in the new generation of detectives!'

Japp grinned more widely.

'I don't know,' he said. 'Miller, the man who's on this case, is a smart chap. You may be very sure he won't overlook a footprint, or cigar ash, or a crumb even. He's got eyes that see everything.'

'So, my friend,' said Poirot, 'has the London sparrow. But all the same, I should not ask the little brown bird to solve the problem of Mr Davenheim.'

'Come now, monsieur, you're not going to run down the value of details as clues?'

'By no means. These things are all good in their way. The danger is they may be seen as too important. Most details are of no interest; one or two are vital. It is the brain, the little grey cells,' – he tapped his forehead – 'on which one must rely. The senses mislead. One must seek the truth within – not without.'

'You don't mean, Monsieur Poirot, that you would try to solve a case without moving from your chair, do you?'

'That is exactly what I do mean – as long as the facts were placed before me.'

Japp slapped his knee. 'All right then. Let's see if you can do it. I bet you a fiver that you can't find – or rather tell me where to find – Mr Davenheim, dead or alive, before a week is out.'

Poirot considered. 'All right, my friend, I accept. Games are a passion of you English. Now – the facts.'

'Last Saturday, as usual,' Japp began, 'Mr Davenheim took the 12.40 train from Victoria to Chingside, where he has a country house which is more like a palace, called The Cedars. After lunch, he strolled round the grounds, and spoke to the gardeners. Everybody agrees that his manner was absolutely normal and as usual. After tea he put his head into his wife's room, saying that he was going to stroll down to the village and post some letters. He added that he was expecting a Mr Lowen, on business. If he should come before he himself returned, he was to be shown into the study and asked to wait. Mr Davenheim then left the house by the front door, passed leisurely down the drive, and out at the gate, and – was never seen again. From that hour, he vanished completely.'

'Pretty – very pretty – altogether a charming little problem,' murmured Poirot. 'Proceed, my good friend.'

'About a quarter of an hour later a tall, dark man with a thick black moustache rang the front doorbell at The Cedars, and explained that he had an appointment with Mr Davenheim. He gave the name of Lowen, and as the banker had instructed was shown into the study. Nearly an hour passed. Mr Davenheim did not return. Finally Mr Lowen rang the bell, and explained that he was unable to wait any longer, as he must catch his train back to town.

'Mrs Davenheim apologized for her husband's absence, which she couldn't explain, as she knew that he had been expecting the visitor. Mr Lowen said again that he was sorry and left.

'Well, as everyone knows, Mr Davenheim did *not* return. Early on Sunday morning the police were called, but could make no sense of the matter. Mr Davenheim seemed to have vanished into thin air. He had not been to the post office; nor had he been seen passing through the village. At the station they were certain he had not departed by any train. His own car had not left the garage. If he had hired a car to meet him in some lonely spot, it seems almost certain that by now, in view of the large reward offered for information, the driver of it would have come forward to tell what he knew. True, there was a small race meeting at Entfield, five miles away, and if he had walked to that station he might have passed unnoticed in the crowd. But since then his photograph and a full description of him have been circulated in every newspaper, and nobody has been able to give any news of him. We have, of course, received many letters from all over England, but each clue, so far, has led nowhere.

'On Monday morning a further sensational discovery was made. Behind a heavy curtain in Mr Davenheim's study stands a safe, and that safe had been broken into and looted. The windows were fastened securely on the inside, which seems to rule out an ordinary burglary, unless, of course, an accomplice within the house fastened them again afterwards. On the other hand, on Sunday the household was in a state of chaos, so it is likely that the burglary was committed on the Saturday, and remained undetected until Monday.'

'Precisely,' said Poirot dryly. 'Well, is he arrested, this poor Mr Lowen?'

Japp grinned. 'Not yet. But he's under pretty close supervision.'

Poirot nodded. 'What was taken from the safe? Have you any idea?'

'We've been going into that with the junior partner of the firm and Mrs Davenheim. Apparently there was a large amount of money in bonds, and a very large sum in notes, owing to some large transaction having been just carried through. There was also a small fortune in jewellery. All Mrs Davenheim's jewels were kept in the safe. Buying jewellery had become a passion with her husband in recent years, and hardly a month passed when he did not make her a present of some rare and costly gem.'

'Altogether a good haul,' said Poirot thoughtfully. 'Now, what about Lowen? Is it known what his business was with Davenheim that evening?'

'Well, the two men were apparently not on very good terms. Lowen invests in stocks and shares in quite a small way. But he has been able once or twice to score a coup off Davenheim in the market, though it seems they seldom or never actually met. It was a matter concerning some South American shares which led the banker to make the appointment.'

'Had Davenheim interests in South America, then?'

'I believe so. Mrs Davenheim mentioned that he spent all last autumn in Buenos Aires.'

'Any trouble in his home life? Were the husband and wife on good terms?'

'I should say his domestic life was quite peaceful and uneventful. Mrs Davenheim is a pleasant, not very bright woman. A bit of a nobody, I think.'

'Then we must not look for the solution of the mystery there. Had he any enemies?'

'He had plenty of financial rivals, and no doubt there are many people whom he has got the better of who don't like him much. But there was no one likely to kill him – and, if they had, where is the body?'

'Exactly. As Hastings says, bodies have a habit of coming to light.'

'By the way, one of the gardeners says he saw someone going round to the side of the house towards the rose garden. The long french window of the study opens on to the rose garden, and Mr Davenheim frequently entered and left the house that way. But the man was a good way off, at work on some cucumber frames, and cannot even say whether it was Mr Davenheim or not. Also, he cannot fix the time with any accuracy. It must have been before six, as the gardeners stop work then.'

'And Mr Davenheim left the house?'

'About half-past five.'

'What lies beyond the rose garden?'

'A lake.'

'With a boathouse?'

'Yes, a couple of punts are kept there. I suppose you're thinking of suicide, Monsieur Poirot? Well, I don't mind telling you that Miller's going down tomorrow expressly to see that piece of water dragged. That's the kind of man he is!'

Poirot smiled faintly, and turned to me. 'Hastings, please hand me that copy of *Daily Megaphone*. If I remember rightly, there is an unusually clear photograph there of the missing man.'

I rose, and found the paper. Poirot studied the features attentively.

'H'm!' he murmured. 'Wears his hair rather long and wavy, full moustache and pointed beard, bushy eyebrows. Eyes dark?'

'Yes.'

'Hair and beard turning grey?'

The detective nodded. 'Well, Monsieur Poirot, what have you got to say to it all? Clear as daylight, eh?'

'On the contrary, most obscure.'

The Scotland Yard man looked pleased.

'Which gives me great hopes of solving it,' said Poirot quietly.

'Eh?'

'I find it a good sign when a case is obscure. If a thing is clear as daylight – well, mistrust it! Someone has made it so.'

Japp shook his head almost with pity. 'Well, each to his own. But it's not a bad thing to see your way clear ahead.'

'I do not see,' murmured Poirot. 'I shut my eyes – and think.'

Japp sighed. 'Well, you've got a clear week to think in.'

'And you will bring me any fresh facts that arise – the result of the labours of the hard-working and lynx-eyed Inspector Miller, for instance?'

'Certainly. That's in the bargain.'

'Seems a shame, doesn't it?' said Japp to me as I went with him to the door. 'Like robbing a child!'

I could not help agreeing with a smile. I was still smiling as I came back into the room.

'Well!' said Poirot immediately. 'You make fun of Papa Poirot, is it not so?' He shook his finger at me. 'You do not trust his grey cells? Ah, do not be confused! Let us discuss this little problem – incomplete as yet, I admit, but already showing one or two points of interest.'

'The lake!' I said firmly.

'And even more than the lake, the boathouse!'

I looked sideways at Poirot. He was smiling in his most inscrutable fashion. I felt that, for the moment, it would be quite useless to question him further.

We heard nothing of Japp until the following evening, when he walked in about nine o'clock. I saw at once by his expression that he was bursting with news of some kind.

'Well, my friend,' remarked Poirot. 'All goes well? But do not tell me that you have discovered the body of Mr Davenheim in your lake, because I shall not believe you.'

'We haven't found the body, but we did find his *clothes* – the identical clothes he was wearing that day. What do you say to that?'

'Any other clothes missing from the house?'

'No, his valet was quite positive on that point. The rest of his clothes are where they should be. There's more. We've arrested Lowen. One of the maids, whose job is to fasten the bedroom

31

windows, declares that she saw Lowen coming *towards* the study through the rose garden about a quarter past six. That would be about ten minutes before he left the house.'

'What does he himself say to that?'

'Denied first of all that he had ever left the study. But the maid was positive, and then he pretended that he had forgotten just stepping out of the window to examine an unusual species of rose. Rather a weak story! And there's fresh evidence against him. Mr Davenheim always wore a thick gold ring set with a solitaire diamond on the little finger of his right hand. Well, that ring was pawned in London on Saturday night by a man called Billy Kellett!

'Kellett is already known to the police – did three months last autumn for lifting an old gentleman's watch. It seems he tried to pawn the ring at no less than five different places, succeeded at the last one, got very drunk on the proceeds, assaulted a policeman, and was arrested. I went to Bow Street with Miller and saw him. He's sober enough now, and I don't mind admitting we pretty well frightened the life out of him, hinting he might be charged with murder. This is his story, and a very queer one it is.

'He was at Entfield races on Saturday, though I dare say stealing scarf pins was his line of business, rather than betting. Anyway, he had a bad day, and was down on his luck. He was tramping along the road to Chingside, and sat down in a ditch to rest just before he got into the village. A few minutes later he noticed a man coming along the road to the village, "dark-complexioned gent, with a big moustache, one of them city toffs," is his description of the man.

'Kellett was half concealed from the road by a heap of stones. Just before he got abreast of him, the man looked quickly up and down the road, and seeing it apparently deserted he took a small object from his pocket and threw it over the hedge. Then he went on towards the station. Now, the object he had thrown over the hedge had fallen with a slight "chink" which attracted Kellett as he sat in the ditch. He went to look and, after a short search, found the ring! That is Kellett's story. It's only fair to say that Lowen denies it utterly, and of course the word of a man like Kellett can't be relied upon in the slightest. It's within the bounds of possibility that he met Davenheim in the lane and robbed and murdered him.'

Poirot shook his head.

'Very unlikely, my friend. He had no means of disposing of the body. It would have been found by now. Secondly, the open way in which he pawned the ring makes it unlikely that he did murder to get it. Thirdly, your sneak-thief is rarely a murderer. Fourthly, as he has been in prison since Saturday, it would be too much of a coincidence that he is able to give so accurate a description of Lowen.'

Japp nodded. 'I don't say you're not right. But all the same, you won't get a jury to take much note of a jailbird's evidence. What seems odd to me is that Lowen couldn't find a cleverer way of disposing of the ring.'

Poirot shrugged his shoulders. 'Well, after all, if it were found in the neighbourhood, it might be argued that Davenheim himself had dropped it.'

'But why remove it from the body at all?' I cried.

'There might be a reason for that,' said Japp. 'Do you know that just beyond the lake, a little gate leads out on to the hill, and not three minutes' walk brings you to – what do you think? – a *lime kiln*.'

'Good heavens!' I cried. 'You mean that the lime which destroyed the body would be powerless to affect the metal of the ring?'

'Exactly.'

'It seems to me,' I said, 'that that explains everything. What a horrible crime!'

By common consent we both turned and looked at Poirot. He seemed lost in reflection, his forehead creased, as though with some supreme mental effort. I felt at last his keen intellect was coming to life. What would his first words be? We were not long left in doubt. With a sigh, the tension of his attitude relaxed and turning to Japp, he asked:

'Have you any idea, my friend, whether Mr and Mrs Davenheim occupied the same bedroom?'

The question seemed so ludicrously odd that for a moment we both stared in silence. Then Japp burst into a laugh. 'Good Lord, Monsieur Poirot, I thought you were coming out with something startling. As to your question, I'm sure I don't know.'

'You could find out?' asked Poirot with curious persistence.

'Oh, certainly – if you *really* want to know.'

'Thank you, my friend. I should be obliged if you would make a point of it.'

Japp stared at him a few minutes longer, but Poirot seemed to have forgotten us both. The Scotland Yard detective shook his head sadly at me, and murmuring, 'Poor old fellow! War's been too much for him!' gently withdrew from the room.

As Poirot seemed sunk in a daydream, I took a sheet of paper, and amused myself by scribbling notes upon it. My friend's voice aroused me. He had come out of his dream, and was looking brisk and alert.

'What are you doing, my friend?'

'I was jotting down what occurred to me as the main points of interest in this affair.'

'You become methodical – at last!' said Poirot happily.

I hid my pleasure. 'Shall I read them to you?'

'By all means.'

I cleared my throat.

'"One: All the evidence points to Lowen having been the man who forced the safe.

'"Two: He had a grudge against Davenheim.

'"Three: He lied in his first statement that he had never left the study.

'"Four: If you accept Billy Kellett's story as true, Lowen is unmistakably implicated."'

I paused. 'Well?' I asked, for I felt that I had put my finger on all the vital facts.

Poirot looked at me with pity, shaking his head very gently. 'My poor friend! You have not the gift! The important detail, you don't see it ever! Also, your reasoning is false.'

'How?'

'Let me take your four points. One: Mr Lowen could not possibly know that he would have the chance to open the safe. He came for a business interview. He could not know beforehand that Mr Davenheim would be absent posting a letter, and that he would therefore be alone in the study!'

'He might have seized the opportunity,' I suggested.

'And the tools? City gentlemen do not carry round housebreaker's tools on the off chance! And one could not cut into that safe with a penknife, of course!'

'Well, what about Number Two?'

'You say Lowen had a grudge against Mr Davenheim. What you mean is that he had once or twice got the better of him. And we presume that those deals were to his benefit. In any case you do not as a rule bear a grudge against a man you have got the better of – it is more likely to be the other way about. Whatever grudge there might have been would have been on Mr Davenheim's side.'

'Well, you can't deny that he lied about never having left the study?'

'No. But he may have been frightened. Remember, when Lowen was questioned, the missing man's clothes had just been discovered in the lake. Of course, as usual, he would have done better to speak the truth.'

'And the fourth point?'

'I grant you that. If Kellett's story is true, Lowen is undeniably implicated. That is what makes the affair so very interesting.'

'Then I *did* appreciate one vital fact?'

'Perhaps – but you have entirely overlooked the two most important points, the ones which undoubtedly hold the clue to the whole matter.'

'And pray, what are they?'

'One, the passion which has grown upon Mr Davenheim in the last few years for buying jewellery. Two, his trip to Buenos Aires last autumn.'

'Poirot, you are joking?'

'I am serious. Ah, sacred thunder! I hope Japp will not forget my little question.'

But the detective, entering into the spirit of the joke, had remembered it so well that a telegram was handed to Poirot about eleven o'clock the next day. At his request I opened it and read it out:

'"Husband and wife have occupied separate rooms since last winter."'

'Aha!' cried Poirot. 'And now we are in mid June! All is solved!'

I stared at him.

'You have no money in the bank of Davenheim and Salmon, my friend?'

'No,' I said wondering. 'Why?'

'Because I should advise you to withdraw it – before it is too late.'

'Why, what do you expect?'

'I expect a big smash in a few days – perhaps sooner. Which reminds me, we will return the compliment of a telegram to Japp. A pencil please, and a form. There! "Advise you to withdraw any money deposited with firm in question." That will intrigue him, the good Japp! His eyes will open wide – wide! He will not understand this at all – until tomorrow, or the next day!'

I was not sure, but the next morning I was forced to wonder at my friend's remarkable powers. In every paper was a huge headline telling of the sensational failure of the Davenheim bank. The disappearance of the famous banker appeared totally different in the light of this news.

Before we were halfway through breakfast, the door flew open and Japp rushed in. In his left hand was a paper; in his right was Poirot's telegram, which he banged down on the table in front of my friend.

'How did you know, Monsieur Poirot? How the blazes could you know?'

Poirot smiled at him calmly. 'Ah, my friend, after your telegram, it was a certainty! From the start, you see, it struck me that the safe burglary was somewhat remarkable. Jewels, ready money, bonds – all so conveniently arranged for – whom?

'Well, the good Monsieur Davenheim was one of those who "look after Number One" as your saying goes! It seemed almost certain that it was arranged for – himself! Then his passion of late years for buying jewellery! How simple! The funds he stole, he turned into jewels, very likely replacing them in turn with paste copies. So he put away in a safe place, under another name, a large fortune to be enjoyed in the future when everyone has been thrown off the track.

'His plans complete, he makes an appointment with Mr Lowen (who has been foolish enough in the past to cross the great man once or twice), drills a hole in the safe, leaves orders that the guest is to be shown into the study, and walks out of the house – where?' Poirot stopped, and stretched out his hand for another boiled egg. He frowned. 'It is really dreadful,' he murmured, 'that every hen lays an egg of a different size! What symmetry can there be on the breakfast table? At least they should sort them in dozens at the shop!'

'Never mind the eggs,' said Japp impatiently. 'Let 'em lay 'em square if they like. Tell us where the man went to when he left The Cedars – that is, if you know!'

'All right, he went to his hiding place. Ah, this Monsieur Davenheim, there may be something wrong with his grey cells, but they are of the first quality!'

'Do you know where he is hiding?'

'Certainly! It is most ingenious.'

'For the Lord's sake, tell us, then!'

Poirot gently collected every fragment of shell from his plate, placed them in the egg cup, and put the empty eggshell upside down on top of them. This little job done, he smiled at the neat effect, and then beamed fondly at us both.

'Come, my friends, you are men of intelligence. Ask yourself the question I asked myself. "If I were this man, where should *I* hide?" Hastings, what do you say?'

'Well,' I said, 'I think I'd not do a bolt at all. I'd stay in London – in the heart of things, travel by tubes and buses; ten to one I'd never be recognized. There's safety in a crowd.'

Poirot turned to Japp.

'I don't agree,' Japp said. 'Get clear away at once – that's the only chance. I would have had plenty of time to prepare things. I'd have a yacht waiting, with steam up, and I'd be off to one of the most out-of-the-way corners of the world before anyone came looking for me!'

We both looked at Poirot. 'What do *you* say, monsieur?'

For a moment he remained silent. Then a very curious smile flitted across his face.

'My friends, if *I* were hiding from the police, do you know *where* I should hide? *In a prison!*'

'*What?*'

'You are seeking Monsieur Davenheim in order to put him in prison, so you never dream of looking to see if he may not be already there!'

'What do you mean?'

'You tell me Mrs Davenheim is not a very intelligent woman. But I think if you took her up to Bow Street and showed her the man Billy Kellett she would recognize him! In spite of the fact that he has shaved his beard and moustache and those bushy eyebrows, and has cropped his hair close. A woman nearly always knows her husband, though the rest of the world may be fooled.'

'Billy Kellett? But he's known to the police!'

'Did I not tell you Davenheim was a clever man? He prepared his disappearance long beforehand. He was not in Buenos Aires last autumn – he was creating the character of Billy Kellett, "doing three months", so that the police should have no doubts when the time came. He was playing, remember, for a large fortune, as well as liberty. It was worthwhile doing the thing thoroughly. Only –'

'Yes?'

'Well, after his three months in prison he had to wear a false beard and wig, had to *make up as himself again*, and to sleep with a false beard is not easy – it is easily detected! He cannot risk continuing to share the bedroom with his wife. You found out for me that for the last six months, or ever since his supposed return from Buenos Aires, he and Mrs Davenheim occupied separate rooms. Then I was sure!

'Everything fitted in. The gardener who fancied he saw Mr Davenheim going round to the side of the house was quite right. He went to the boathouse, put on his "tramp" clothes, which you may be sure had been safely hidden from the eyes of his valet, and dropped the others in the lake. He proceeded to carry out his plan by pawning the ring in an obvious manner, and then by assaulting a policeman, getting himself safely into the haven of Bow Street, where nobody would ever dream of looking for him!'

'It's impossible,' murmured Japp.

'Ask Mrs Davenheim,' said my friend, smiling.

The next day a letter lay beside Poirot's plate. He opened it and a five-pound note fluttered out. My friend frowned.

'My God! But what shall I do with it? I have much remorse! Poor Japp! Ah, an idea! We will have a little dinner, we three! That makes me feel better. It was really too easy. I am ashamed. I, who would not rob a child – a thousand curses! My friend, what are you thinking, that you laugh so heartily?'

3

The Double Clue is one of Agatha's shortest stories. It's also one of the cleverest. All of the magic ingredients we expect to find are present – clues, suspects, a baffling mystery and Hercule Poirot. This is one of my favourite Agatha Christie stories for two reasons. First, it contains the first meeting with the wonderful Countess Vera Rossakoff, who is an important figure from Poirot's past. And second, the story's central clue involves language. Many of Agatha's plots feature such clues – where the mystery is solved by focusing on the precise words written or spoken by particular people. This is a brilliant example. Here, it is Russian grammar that leads to Poirot solving the mystery! And the great thing is that readers needn't know a word of Russian in order to appreciate the solution.

Sophie Hannah

The Double Clue

'But above everything – no publicity,' said Mr Marcus Hardman for perhaps the fourteenth time.

The word *publicity* occurred regularly in Mr Hardman's conversation. He was a small man, delicately plump, with manicured hands and a gloomy tenor voice. In his way, he was somewhat of a celebrity and the fashionable life was his profession.

He was rich, but not remarkably so, and he spent his money eagerly in the pursuit of social pleasure. His hobby was collecting. He had the collector's soul. Old lace, old fans, antique jewellery – nothing crude or modern for Marcus Hardman.

Poirot and I were urgently requested to visit the little man. We had arrived to find him upset and unsure what to do. To call in the police was against his nature. On the other hand, not to call them in was to accept the loss of some of the gems of his collection. He had thought of Poirot as a compromise.

'My rubies, Monsieur Poirot, and the emerald necklace said to have belonged to Catherine dé Medici, the legendary Queen of France. Oh, the emerald necklace!'

'If you will tell me how they came to disappear?' suggested Poirot gently.

'I am trying to do so. Yesterday afternoon I had a little tea party – quite an informal affair, some half a dozen people or so. I have given one or two of them during the season, and though perhaps I should not say so, they have been quite a success. Some good music – Nacora, the pianist, and Katherine Bird, the Australian contralto – in the big studio.

'Well, early in the afternoon, I was showing my guests my collection of medieval jewels. I keep them in the small wall safe over there. It is arranged like a cabinet inside, with coloured velvet background, to display the stones. Afterwards we inspected the fans – in the case on the wall. Then we all went to the studio for music.

'It was not until after everyone had gone that I discovered the safe looted! I must have failed to shut it properly, and someone had seized the opportunity to steal its contents. The rubies,

Monsieur Poirot, the emerald necklace – the collection of a lifetime! What would I not give to recover them! But there must be no publicity, nothing in the newspapers! You fully understand that, do you not, Monsieur Poirot? My own guests, my personal friends! It would be a horrible scandal!'

'Who was the last person to leave this room when you went to the studio?'

'Mr Johnston. You may know him? The South African millionaire. He has just rented the Abbotburys' house in Park Lane. He lingered behind a few moments, I remember. But surely, oh, surely it could not be he!'

'Did any of your guests return to this room during the afternoon on any pretext?'

'I was prepared for that question, Monsieur Poirot. Three of them did. Countess Vera Rossakoff, Mr Bernard Parker, and Lady Runcorn.'

'Let us hear about them.'

'The Countess Rossakoff is a very charming Russian lady, a member of the old regime. She has recently come to this country. She had said goodbye to me, and I was therefore somewhat surprised to find her in this room apparently gazing in rapture at my cabinet of fans. You know, Monsieur Poirot, the more I think of it, the more suspicious it seems to me. Don't you agree?'

'Extremely suspicious; but let us hear about the others.'

'Well, Parker simply came here to fetch a case of miniature portraits that I was anxious to show to Lady Runcorn.'

'And Lady Runcorn herself?'

'As I dare say you know, Lady Runcorn is a middle-aged woman of strong character who devotes most of her time to charitable work. She simply returned to fetch a handbag she had laid down somewhere.'

'Well, monsieur. So we have four possible suspects. The Russian countess, the grand English lady, the South African millionaire, and Mr Bernard Parker. Who *is* Mr Parker, by the way?'

The question appeared to embarrass Mr Hardman a great deal.

'He is – er – he is a young fellow. Well, in fact, a young fellow I know.'

'I had already deduced as much,' replied Poirot gravely. 'What does he do, this Mr Parker?'

'He is a young man about town – not, perhaps, one of my usual circle of friends, if I may so express myself.'

'How did he come to be a friend, may I ask?'

'Well – er – on one or two occasions he has – performed certain little jobs for me.'

'Continue, monsieur,' said Poirot.

Hardman looked at him sheepishly. Evidently the last thing he wanted to do was to continue. But as Poirot remained totally silent, he had no choice.

'You see, Monsieur Poirot – it is well known that I am interested in antique jewels. Sometimes someone wants to sell a family heirloom – which, mind you, would never be sold in the open market or to a dealer.

'But a private sale to me is a very different matter. Parker arranges the details of such things, he is in touch with both sides, and thus any little embarrassment is avoided. He brings anything of that kind to my notice.

'For instance, the Countess Rossakoff has brought some family jewels with her from Russia. She is keen to sell them. Bernard Parker was to have arranged the sale.'

'I see,' said Poirot thoughtfully. 'And you trust him completely?'

'I have had no reason not to.'

'Mr Hardman, of these four people, which do you yourself suspect?'

'Oh, Monsieur Poirot, what a question! They are my friends, as I told you. I suspect none of them – or all of them, whichever way you like to put it.'

'I do not agree. You suspect one of those four. It is not Countess Rossakoff. It is not Mr Parker. Is it Lady Runcorn or Mr Johnston?'

'You drive me into a corner, Monsieur Poirot, you do indeed. I am most keen to have no scandal. Lady Runcorn belongs to one of the oldest families in England; but it is true, it is most unfortunately true, that her aunt, Lady Caroline, suffered from a very sad affliction. It was understood, of course, by all her friends, and her maid returned the teaspoons, or whatever it was, as promptly as possible. You see my problem!'

'So Lady Runcorn had an aunt who was a kleptomaniac? Very interesting. Will you let me examine the safe?'

Mr Hardman agreeing, Poirot pushed back the door of the safe and examined the inside. The empty velvet-lined shelves gaped at us.

'Even now the door does not shut properly,' murmured Poirot, as he swung it to and fro. 'I wonder why? Ah, what have we here? A glove, caught in the hinge. A man's glove.'

He held it out to Mr Hardman.

'That's not one of my gloves,' the latter declared.

'Aha! Something more!' Poirot bent deftly and picked up a small object from the floor of the safe. It was a flat cigarette case made of black moiré.

'My cigarette case!' cried Mr Hardman.

'Yours? Surely not, monsieur. Those are not your initials.'

He pointed to a monogram of two letters made with platinum.

Hardman took it in his hand.

'You are right,' he declared. 'It is very like mine, but the initials are different. A *"B"* and a *"P"*. Good heavens – Parker!'

'It would seem so,' said Poirot. 'A somewhat careless young man – especially if the glove is his also. That would be a double clue, would it not?'

'Bernard Parker!' murmured Hardman. 'What a relief! Well, Monsieur Poirot, I leave it to you to recover the jewels. Place the matter in the hands of the police if you think fit – that is, if you are quite sure that it is he who is guilty.'

'See you, my friend,' said Poirot to me, as we left the house together, 'he has one law for the titled, and another law for the plain, this Mr Hardman. Me, I have not yet been given a title, so I am on the side of the plain. I feel for this young man. The whole thing was a little curious, was it not? There was Hardman suspecting Lady Runcorn; there was I, suspecting the Countess and Johnston; and all the time, the obscure Mr Parker was our man.'

'Why did you suspect the other two?'

'Heavens! It is such a simple thing to be a Russian refugee or a South African millionaire. Any woman can call herself a Russian countess; anyone can buy a house in Park Lane and call himself a South African millionaire. Who is going to contradict them? But I see that we are passing through Bury Street. Our careless young friend lives here. Let us, as you say, strike while the iron is hot.'

Mr Bernard Parker was at home. We found him lounging on some cushions, dressed in an amazing dressing gown of purple and orange. I have seldom taken a greater dislike to anyone than I did to this young man with his white, effeminate face and phoney lisping speech.

'Good morning, monsieur,' said Poirot briskly. 'I come from Mr Hardman. Yesterday, at the party, somebody has stolen all his jewels. Permit me to ask you, monsieur – is this your glove?'

Mr Parker's brain seemed to work slowly. He stared at the glove, as though gathering his wits together.

'Where did you find it?' he asked at last.

'Is it your glove, monsieur?'

Mr Parker appeared to make up his mind.

'No, it isn't,' he declared.

'And this cigarette case, is that yours?'

'Certainly not. I always carry a silver one.'

'Very well, monsieur. I go to put matters in the hands of the police.'

'Oh, I say, I wouldn't do that if I were you,' cried Mr Parker in some concern. 'Beastly unkind people, the police. Wait a bit. I'll go round and see old Hardman. Look here – oh, stop a minute.'

But Poirot left quickly and said no more.

'We have given him something to think about, have we not?' he chuckled. 'Tomorrow we will see what has occurred.'

But we were reminded of the Hardman case that afternoon. Without warning the door flew open, and a human whirlwind came in, bringing with her a swirl of furs (it was as cold as only an English June day can be) and a hat decked out with dead ospreys. Countess Vera Rossakoff was a somewhat disturbing person.

'You are Monsieur Poirot? What is this that you have done? You accuse that poor boy! It is vile. It is scandalous. I know him. He is a chicken, a lamb – never would he steal. He has done everything for me. Will I stand by and see him killed and butchered?'

'Tell me, madam, is this his cigarette case?' Poirot held out the black moiré case.

The Countess paused for a moment while she inspected it.

'Yes, it is his. I know it well. What of it? Did you find it in the room? We were all there; he dropped it then, I suppose. Ah, you policemen, you are worse than the Russian Red Guards –'

'And is this his glove?'

'How should I know? One glove is like another. Do not try to stop me – he must be set free. His character must be cleared. You shall do it. I will sell my jewels and give you much money.'

'Madam –'

'It is agreed, then? No, no, do not argue. The poor boy! He came to me, the tears in his eyes. "I will save you," I said. "I will go to this man – this brute, this monster! Leave it to Vera." Now it is settled, I go.'

Without saying goodbye, she swept from the room, leaving an overpowering perfume of an exotic nature behind her.

'What a woman!' I shouted. 'And what furs!'

'Ah, yes, *they* were real enough. Could a fake countess have real furs? My little joke, Hastings . . . No, she is truly Russian, I think. Well, well, so Master Bernard went bleating to her.'

'The cigarette case is his. I wonder if the glove is also –'

With a smile Poirot drew from his pocket a second glove and placed it by the first. There was no doubt that they were a pair.

'Where did you get the second one, Poirot?'

'It was thrown down with a stick on the table in the hall in Bury Street. Truly, a very careless young man, Mr Parker. Well, well, my friend – we must be thorough. Just for the form of the thing, I will make a little visit to Park Lane.'

Of course, I accompanied my friend. Johnston was out, but we saw his private secretary. It turned out that Johnston had only recently arrived from South Africa. He had never been in England before.

'He is interested in precious stones, is he not?' asked Poirot.

'Gold mining is nearer the mark,' laughed the secretary.

Poirot came away from the interview thoughtful. Late that evening, to my utter surprise, I found him earnestly studying a book of Russian grammar.

'Good heavens, Poirot!' I cried. 'Are you learning Russian in order to speak to the Countess in her own language?'

'She certainly would not listen to my English, my friend!'

'But surely, Poirot, well-born Russians always speak French?'

'You know so many things, Hastings! I will stop puzzling over the Russian alphabet.'

He threw the book from him with a dramatic gesture. I was not entirely satisfied. There was a twinkle in his eye which I knew of old. It was always a sign that Hercule Poirot was pleased with himself.

'Perhaps,' I said sharply, 'you doubt her being really a Russian. You are going to test her?'

'Ah, no, no, she is Russian all right.'

'Well, then –'

'If you really want to succeed with this case, Hastings, I recommend *First Steps in Russian* as a vital aid.'

Then he laughed and would say no more. I picked up the book from the floor and dipped into it curiously, but could make no sense of Poirot's remarks.

The following morning brought us no news of any kind, but that did not seem to worry my little friend. At breakfast, he announced that he would call upon Mr Hardman early in the day. We found the old man at home, and seemingly a little calmer than on the previous day.

'Well, Monsieur Poirot, any news?' he asked eagerly.

Poirot handed him a slip of paper.

'That is the person who took the jewels, monsieur. Shall I put matters in the hands of the police? Or would you prefer me to recover the jewels without bringing the police into the matter?'

Mr Hardman was staring at the paper. At last he managed to speak.

'Most astonishing. I should prefer to have no scandal in the matter. Deal with it as you think best, Monsieur Poirot. I am sure you will be discreet.'

Outside we hailed a taxi, which Poirot ordered to drive to the Carlton. There he asked for Countess Rossakoff. In a few minutes we were led into the lady's suite. She came to meet us with open arms, dressed in a marvellous dressing gown of barbaric design.

'Monsieur Poirot!' she cried. 'You have succeeded? You have cleared that poor infant?'

'Madame la Comtesse, your friend Mr Parker is perfectly safe from arrest.'

'Ah, but you are the clever little man! Superb! And so quickly too.'

'On the other hand, I have promised Mr Hardman that the jewels shall be returned to him today.'

'So?'

'Therefore, madam, I should be extremely grateful if you would place them in my hands without delay. I am sorry to hurry you, but I am keeping a taxi waiting – in case I need to go on to Scotland Yard; and we Belgians, madam, we like to be thrifty.'

The Countess had lit a cigarette. For some seconds she sat perfectly still, blowing smoke rings, and gazing steadily at Poirot. Then she burst into a laugh, and rose. She went across to a bureau, opened a drawer, and took out a black silk handbag. She tossed it lightly to Poirot. Her tone, when she spoke, was perfectly light and unmoved.

'We Russians, on the contrary, are extravagant,' she said. 'And so, unfortunately, one must have money. You need not look inside. They are all there.'

Poirot stood up.

'I congratulate you, madam, on your quick intelligence and your speedy action.'

'Ah! But since you were keeping your taxi waiting, what else could I do?'

'You are too kind, madam. Are you staying long in London?'

'I am afraid no – because of you.'

'Accept my apologies.'

'We shall meet again elsewhere, perhaps.'

'I hope so.'

'And I – do not!' said the Countess with a laugh. 'It is a great compliment that I pay you there – there are very few men in the world whom I fear. Goodbye, Monsieur Poirot.'

'Goodbye, Madame la Comtesse. Ah – pardon me, I forgot! Allow me to return your cigarette case.'

And with a bow he handed to her the little black moiré case we had found in the safe. She took it without any change of expression – just a lifted eyebrow and a murmured: 'I see!'

'What a woman!' cried Poirot joyfully as we descended the stairs. 'My God, what a woman!!

Not a word of argument – of protest, of bluff! One quick glance, and she had sized up the position correctly. I tell you, Hastings, a woman who can accept defeat like that – with a careless smile – will go far! She is dangerous, she has the nerves of steel; she –'

He tripped heavily.

'If you can manage to tread carefully and look where you're going, it might be as well,' I suggested. 'When did you first suspect the Countess?'

'My friend, it was the glove *and* the cigarette case – the double clue, shall we say – that worried me. Bernard Parker might easily have dropped one or the other – but hardly both. Ah, no, that would have been *too* careless! In the same way, if someone else had placed them there to frame Parker, one would have been enough – the cigarette case *or* the glove – again not both.

'So I decided that one of the two things did *not* belong to Parker. I thought at first that the case was his, and that the glove was not. But when I found the pair to the glove, I saw that it was the other way about.

'Whose, then, was the cigarette case? Clearly, it could not belong to Lady Runcorn. The initials were wrong. Mr Johnston? Only if he were here under a false name. I spoke to his secretary, and it was apparent at once that everything was clear and above board. There was nothing murky about Mr Johnston's past.

'The Countess, then? She was supposed to have brought jewels with her from Russia. She had only to take Hardman's rubies and emeralds from their settings, and they would be very unlikely ever to be identified. What could be easier for her than to pick up one of Parker's gloves from the hall that day and thrust it into the safe? But, of course, she did not intend to drop her own cigarette case.'

'But if the case was hers, why did it have "*B.P.*" on it? The Countess's initials are *V.R.*'

Poirot smiled gently upon me.

'Exactly, my friend; but in the Russian alphabet, *B* is *V* and *P* is *R*.'

'Well, you couldn't expect me to guess that. I don't know Russian.'

'Neither do I, Hastings. That is why I bought my little book – and urged you to look at it.'

He sighed.

'A remarkable woman. I have a feeling, my friend – a very definite feeling – I shall meet her again. Where, I wonder?'

4

The Adventure of the Egyptian Tomb was first published in March 1923. Egypt was in the news after the discovery the year before of the tomb and vast treasure trove of the Egyptian King Tutankhamun. When some of the team that made the discovery died shortly afterwards, a rumour began that the tomb was cursed. Agatha Christie used this idea as the basis for her story. But when Hercule Poirot investigates the mysterious deaths that follow the opening of another tomb, he finds that the reasons behind these crimes are as old as time. Poirot was one of only a few fictional detectives to go abroad: Egypt, Mesopotamia, France, Switzerland, Italy, Belgium, Ireland. This reflected Agatha Christie's own love of foreign travel and she put it to good use in many of her novels and stories.

John Curran

The Adventure of the
Egyptian Tomb

I have always thought that one of the most thrilling and dramatic of the many adventures I have shared with Poirot was our investigation into the strange series of deaths that followed upon the discovery and opening of the Tomb of King Men-her-Ra.

Soon after the discovery of the Tomb of Tutankhamun by Lord Carnarvon, Sir John Willard and Mr Bleibner of New York discovered a series of funeral chambers not far from Cairo, near the Pyramids of Giza. The Tomb appeared to be that of King Men-her-Ra, one of those shadowy kings of the Eighth Dynasty, which ruled Egypt in the 21st Century B.C. when the Old Kingdom was falling to decay. Little was known about this period. The discoveries were fully reported in the newspapers and great interest was shown.

An event soon occurred which made a big

impact on the public. Sir John Willard died quite suddenly of heart failure.

The more sensational newspapers immediately revived all the old superstitious stories connected with the ill luck of certain Egyptian treasures. The old story of the unlucky Mummy at the British Museum was dragged out with new relish, was quietly denied by the Museum, but once again became a fad.

A fortnight later Mr Bleibner died of acute blood poisoning, and a few days afterwards a nephew of his shot himself in New York. The 'Curse of Men-her-Ra' was the talk of the day, and belief in the magic power of dead-and-gone Egypt reached an all-time high.

It was then that Poirot received a brief note from Lady Willard, widow of the dead archaeologist, asking him to go and see her at her house in Kensington Square. I went with him.

Lady Willard was a tall, thin woman, dressed in deep mourning. Her haggard face clearly showed her recent grief.

'It is kind of you to have come so promptly, Monsieur Poirot.'

'I am at your service, Lady Willard. You wished to consult me?'

'You are, I am aware, a detective, but it is not only as a detective that I wish to consult you.

You are a man of original views, I know. You have imagination, experience of the world. Tell me, Monsieur Poirot, what are your views on the supernatural?'

Poirot waited for a moment before he replied. He seemed to be considering. Finally he said:

'Let us not misunderstand each other, Lady Willard. It is not a general question that you are asking me there. It has a personal angle, doesn't it? You are referring to the death of your late husband?'

'That is so,' she admitted.

'You want me to investigate the details of his death?'

'I want you to find out for me exactly how much is newspaper chatter, and how much may be said to be founded on fact? Three deaths, Monsieur Poirot – each one simple to explain taken by itself, but taken together surely a most strange coincidence, and all within a month of the opening of the tomb! It may be mere superstition, it may be some potent curse from the past that works in ways undreamed of by modern science. The fact remains – three deaths! And I am afraid, Monsieur Poirot, horribly afraid. It may not yet be the end.'

'For whom do you fear?'

'For my son. When the news of my husband's death came I was ill. My son, who has just left

Oxford University, went out there to Egypt. He brought the – the body home, but now he has gone out again, in spite of my prayers and pleading. He is so fascinated by the work that he intends to take his father's place and carry on digging out the funeral chambers. You may think me a foolish woman, but, Monsieur Poirot, I am afraid. Supposing that the spirit of the dead King is not yet at peace? Perhaps to you I seem to be talking nonsense –'

'No, indeed, Lady Willard,' said Poirot quickly. 'I, too, believe in the force of superstition, one of the greatest forces the world has ever known.'

I looked at him in surprise. I had never thought Poirot to be superstitious. But the little man was obviously in earnest.

'What you really demand is that I shall protect your son? I will do my utmost to keep him from harm.'

'Yes, in the ordinary way, but against a super-natural power?'

'In volumes of the Middle Ages, Lady Willard, you will find many ways of defeating black magic. Perhaps they knew more than we moderns with all our boasted science. Now let us come to facts, that I may have guidance. Your husband had always been devoted to the history of ancient Egypt, hadn't he?'

68

'Yes, from his youth upwards. He was one of the greatest living experts on the subject.'

'But Mr Bleibner, I understand, was more or less of an amateur?'

'Oh, quite. He was a very wealthy man who dabbled freely in any subject that happened to take his fancy. My husband managed to interest him in ancient Egypt, and it was his money that was so useful in financing the expedition.'

'And the nephew? What do you know of his tastes? Was he with the party at all?'

'I do not think so. In fact I never knew of him till I read of his death in the paper. I do not think he and Mr Bleibner can have been at all close. He never spoke of having any relations.'

'Who are the other members of the party?'

'Well, there's Dr Tosswill, a minor official from the British Museum; Mr Schneider of the Metropolitan Museum in New York; a young American secretary; Dr Ames, who is the expedition's medic; and Hassan, my husband's devoted native servant.'

'Do you remember the name of the American secretary?'

'Harper, I think, but I cannot be sure. He had not been with Mr Bleibner very long, I know. He was a very pleasant young fellow.'

'Thank you, Lady Willard.'

'If there is anything else –'

'For the moment, nothing. Leave it now in my hands, and be assured that I will do all that is humanly possible to protect your son.'

They were not exactly comforting words, and I saw Lady Willard wince as he spoke them. Yet, at the same time, the fact that he had not pooh-poohed her fears seemed to be a relief to her. For my part, I had never before suspected that Poirot took superstition seriously. I asked him about it as we went home. His manner was grave and earnest.

'But yes, Hastings. I believe in these things. You must not underrate the force of superstition.'

'What are we going to do about it?'

'Always practical, the good Hastings! Well, to begin with we are going to cable to New York for fuller details of young Mr Bleibner's death.'

He duly sent off his cable. The reply was full and precise. Young Rupert Bleibner had been in a bad way for several years. He had been a beachcomber, living off money sent from home, on several South Sea islands, but had returned to New York two years ago, where he had rapidly sunk lower and lower. The most interesting thing, to my mind, was that he had recently borrowed enough money to take him to Egypt. 'I've a good friend there I can borrow from,' he had said. There, however, his plans had gone wrong.

He had returned to New York cursing his skin-flint of an uncle who cared more for the bones of dead kings than his own flesh and blood. It was during his time in Egypt that the death of Sir John Willard had occurred. Rupert had plunged once more into his disreputable life in New York. Then, without warning, he had committed suicide, leaving behind him a letter which contained some curious phrases. It seemed to have been written in a sudden fit of regret. He referred to himself as a leper and an outcast, and the letter ended by declaring that such as he were better dead.

A shadowy theory leapt into my brain. I had never really believed in the revenge of a long-dead Egyptian king. I saw here a more modern crime. Supposing this young man had decided to do away with his uncle – perhaps by poison. By mistake, Sir John Willard receives the fatal dose. The young man returns to New York, haunted by his crime. The news of his uncle's death reaches him. He realizes how pointless his crime has been, and stricken with regret takes his own life.

I outlined my solution to Poirot. He was interested.

'It is ingenious what you have thought of there – decidedly it is ingenious. It may even be true. But you leave out the fatal influence of the Tomb.'

I shrugged my shoulders.

'You still think that has something to do with it?'

'So much so, my friend, that we start for Egypt tomorrow.'

'What?' I cried, astonished.

'I have said it.' An expression of heroism spread over Poirot's face. Then he groaned. 'But oh, the sea! The hateful sea!'

It was a week later. Beneath our feet was the golden sand of the desert. The hot sun poured down overhead. Poirot, utterly miserable, wilted by my side. The little man was not a good traveller. Our four days' voyage from Marseilles had been one long agony to him. He had landed at Alexandria the ghost of his former self. Even his usual neatness had faded away. We had arrived in Cairo and had driven out at once to the Mena House Hotel, right in the shadow of the Pyramids.

The charm of Egypt had got to me. But not to Poirot. Dressed precisely the same as in London, he carried a small clothes brush in his pocket and waged war on the dust which fell on his dark clothing.

'And my boots,' he wailed. 'Look at them, Hastings. My boots, of the neat patent leather, usually so smart and shining. See, the sand is inside them, which is painful, and outside them, which looks dreadful. Also the heat, it causes my moustaches to become limp – but limp!'

'Look at the Sphinx,' I urged. 'Even I can feel the mystery and the charm it gives off.'

Poirot looked at it sadly.

'It has not a happy air,' he declared. 'How could it, half-buried in sand in that untidy fashion. Ah, this cursed sand!'

'Come, now, there's a lot of sand in Belgium,' I reminded him, thinking of a holiday spent at Knocke-sur-mer in the midst of '*The perfect dunes*' as the guide book had phrased it.

'Not in Brussels,' declared Poirot. He gazed at the Pyramids thoughtfully. 'It is true that they, at least, are of a shape solid and geometrical, but their surface is uneven and most unpleasing. And I don't like the palm trees. They don't even plant them in rows!'

I cut short his unhappy mutterings by suggesting that we should start for the camp. We were to ride there on camels, and the beasts were patiently kneeling, waiting for us to mount. Several striking boys led by a talkative guide were in charge of them.

I skip over the image of Poirot on a camel. He started by groaning and wailing and ended by shrieking, gesturing and praying to the Virgin Mary and every Saint in the calendar. In the end, he climbed off, much embarrassed, and finished the journey on a tiny donkey. I must admit that a trotting camel is no joke for the amateur. I was stiff for several days.

At last we came close to the scene of the digging. A sunburnt man with a grey beard, in white clothes and wearing a helmet, came to meet us.

'Monsieur Poirot and Captain Hastings? We received your cable. I'm sorry that there was no one to meet you in Cairo. An unforeseen event occurred which completely wrecked our plans.'

Poirot paled. His hand, which had gone towards his clothes brush, moved no further.

'Not another death?' he breathed.

'Yes.'

'Sir Guy Willard?' I cried.

'No, Captain Hastings. My American colleague, Mr Schneider.'

'And the cause?' demanded Poirot.

'Tetanus.'

I felt myself turn pale. All around me I seemed to feel an atmosphere of evil, subtle and menacing. A horrible thought flashed across me. Supposing I were next?

'My God,' said Poirot, in a very low voice, 'I do not understand this. It is horrible. Tell me, monsieur, there is no doubt that it was tetanus?'

'I believe not. But Dr Ames will tell you more than I can.'

'Ah, of course, you are not the doctor.'

'My name is Tosswill.'

This, then, was the British expert described by Lady Willard as being a minor official at the British Museum. There was something at once grave and steadfast about him that I liked.

'If you will come with me,' continued Dr Tosswill. 'I will take you to Sir Guy Willard. He was most anxious to be informed as soon as you should arrive.'

We were taken across the camp to a large tent. Dr Tosswill lifted up the flap and we entered. Three men were sitting inside.

'Monsieur Poirot and Captain Hastings have arrived, Sir Guy,' said Tosswill.

The youngest of the three men jumped up and came forward to greet us. There was a certain haste in his manner which reminded me of his mother. He was not nearly so sunburnt as the others, and that fact, coupled with a tiredness round the eyes, made him look older than his twenty-two years. He was clearly doing his utmost to bear up under a severe mental strain.

He introduced his two companions, Dr Ames, a capable-looking man of thirty-odd, with a touch of greying hair at the temples, and Mr Harper, the secretary, a pleasant lean young man wearing the national uniform of horn-rimmed spectacles.

After a few minutes' casual conversation Mr Harper went out, and Dr Tosswill followed him. We were left alone with Sir Guy and Dr Ames.

'Please ask any questions you want to ask, Monsieur Poirot,' said Willard. 'We are utterly dumbstruck by this strange series of disasters, but it isn't – it can't be, anything but coincidence.'

There was a nervousness about his manner which seemed at odds with his words. I saw that Poirot was studying him keenly.

'Your heart is really in this work, Sir Guy?'

'Rather. No matter what happens, or what comes of it, the work is going on. You can be sure about that.'

Poirot wheeled round on the other man.

'What have you to say to that, doctor?'

'Well,' drawled the doctor, 'I'm not for quitting myself.'

Poirot pulled one of those expressive faces of his.

'Then, clearly, we must find out just how we stand. When did Mr Schneider's death take place?'

'Three days ago.'

'You are sure it was tetanus?'

'Dead sure.'

'It couldn't have been a case of strychnine poisoning, for instance?'

'No, Monsieur Poirot, I see what you are getting at. But it was a clear case of tetanus.'

'Did you not inject anti-serum?'

'Certainly we did,' said the doctor dryly. 'Every possible thing that could be done was tried.'

'Had you the anti-serum with you?'

'No. We got it from Cairo.'

'Have there been any other cases of tetanus in the camp?'

'No, not one.'

'Are you certain that the death of Mr Bleibner was not due to tetanus?'

'Absolutely plumb certain. He had a scratch upon his thumb which became poisoned, and septicaemia set in. It sounds pretty much the same to a layman, I dare say, but the two things are entirely different.'

'Then we have four deaths – all totally different, one heart failure, one blood poisoning, one suicide and one tetanus.'

'Exactly, Monsieur Poirot.'

'Are you certain that there is nothing which might link the four together?'

'I don't quite understand you?'

'I will put it plainly. Was any act committed by those four men which might seem to show disrespect to the spirit of Men-her-Ra?'

The doctor gazed at Poirot in astonishment.

'You're talking through your hat, Monsieur Poirot. Surely you've not been pushed into believing all that fool talk?'

'Absolute nonsense,' muttered Willard angrily.

Poirot remained quietly immovable, blinking a little out of his green cat's eyes.

'So you do not believe it, doctor?'

'No, sir, I do not,' declared the doctor firmly. 'I am a scientific man, and I believe only what science teaches.'

'Was there no science then in Ancient Egypt?' asked Poirot softly. He did not wait for a reply, and indeed Dr Ames seemed rather at a loss for the moment. 'No, no, do not answer me, but tell me this. What do the native workmen think?'

'I guess,' said Dr Ames, 'that, where white folk lose their reason, natives aren't going to be far behind. I'll admit that they're getting what you might call scared – but they've no cause to be.'

'I wonder,' said Poirot vaguely.

Sir Guy leant forward.

'Surely,' he cried in a shocked voice, 'you cannot believe in – oh, but the thing's absurd! You can know nothing of Ancient Egypt if you think that.'

For answer Poirot produced a little book from his pocket – an ancient tattered volume. As he held it out I saw its title, *The Magic of the Egyptians*

78

and Chaldeans. Then, wheeling round, he strode out of the tent. The doctor stared at me.

'What is his little idea?'

The phrase, often spoken by Poirot, made me smile as it came from another.

'I don't know exactly,' I confessed. 'He's got some plan of exorcizing the evil spirits, I believe.'

I went in search of Poirot, and found him talking to the lean-faced young man who had been the late Mr Bleibner's secretary.

'No,' Mr Harper was saying, 'I've only been six months with the expedition. Yes, I knew Mr Bleibner's affairs pretty well.'

'Can you tell me anything concerning his nephew?'

'He turned up here one day, not a bad-looking fellow. I'd never met him before, but some of the others had – Ames, I think, and Schneider. The old man wasn't at all pleased to see him. They were arguing in no time, strong stuff. "Not a cent," the old man shouted. "Not one cent now or when I'm dead. I intend to leave my money to the furthering of my life's work. I've been talking it over with Mr Schneider today." And a bit more of the same. Young Bleibner lit out for Cairo right away.'

'Was he in perfectly good health at the time?'

'The old man?'

'No, the young one.'

'I believe he did mention there was something wrong with him. But it couldn't have been anything serious, or I should have remembered.'

'One thing more, has Mr Bleibner left a will?'

'So far as we know, he has not.'

'Are you staying with the expedition, Mr Harper?'

'No, sir, I am not. I'm for New York as soon as I can square up things here. You may laugh if you like, but I'm not going to be this blasted Men-her-Ra's next victim. He'll get me if I stop here.'

The young man wiped the sweat from his brow.

Poirot turned away. Over his shoulder he said with a peculiar smile: 'Remember, he got one of his victims in New York.'

'Oh, hell!' said Mr Harper angrily.

'That young man is nervous,' said Poirot thoughtfully. 'He is on the edge, absolutely on the edge.'

I glanced at Poirot curiously, but his enigmatic smile told me nothing. With Sir Guy Willard and Dr Tosswill we were taken round the tombs. The principal finds had been removed to Cairo, but some of the tomb furniture was extremely interesting. The enthusiasm of Sir Guy was obvious, but I felt there was a shade of nervousness in his manner as though he could not quite escape from the feeling of menace in the air.

As we entered the tent which had been assigned to us, for a wash before joining the evening meal, a tall dark figure in white robes stood aside to let us pass with a graceful gesture and a murmured greeting in Arabic. Poirot stopped.

'You are Hassan, the late Sir John Willard's servant?'

'I served my Lord Sir John, now I serve his son.' He took a step nearer to us and lowered his voice. 'You are a wise one, they say, skilled in dealing with evil spirits. Let the young master depart from here. There is evil in the air around us.'

And with an abrupt gesture, not waiting for a reply, he strode away.

'Evil in the air,' muttered Poirot. 'Yes, I feel it.'

Our meal was hardly a cheerful one. Little was said, except by Dr Tosswill, who told us much about Egyptian antiquities. Just as we were preparing to retire to rest, Sir Guy caught Poirot by the arm and pointed. A shadowy figure was moving among the tents. It was no human one: I recognized distinctly the dog-headed figure I had seen carved on the walls of the tomb.

My blood froze at the sight.

'My God!' murmured Poirot, crossing himself vigorously. 'Anubis, the jackal-headed, the god of departing souls.'

81

'Someone is hoaxing us,' cried Dr Tosswill, rising angrily to his feet.

'It went into your tent, Harper,' muttered Sir Guy, his face dreadfully pale.

'No,' said Poirot, shaking his head, 'into that of Dr Ames.'

The doctor stared at him amazed; then, repeating Dr Tosswill's words, he cried: 'Someone is hoaxing us. Come, we'll soon catch the fellow.'

He dashed after the shadowy apparition. I followed him, but, search as we would, we could find no trace of any living soul having passed that way. We returned, somewhat disturbed in mind, to find Poirot taking great trouble, in his own way, to ensure his personal safety. He was busily surrounding our tent with various diagrams and symbols which he was drawing in the sand.

I recognized the five-pointed star or Pentagon many times repeated. As was his way, Poirot was at the same time giving an unplanned lecture on witchcraft and magic in general, White magic as opposed to Black, with references to the Ka and the Book of the Dead thrown in.

This excited the liveliest contempt in Dr Tosswill, who drew me aside, literally snorting with rage.

'Nonsense, sir,' he exclaimed angrily. 'Pure nonsense. The man's an imposter. He doesn't know the difference between the superstitions of the Middle Ages and the beliefs of Ancient Egypt. Never have I heard such a hotchpotch of ignorance and stupidity.'

I calmed the excited expert, and joined Poirot in the tent. My little friend was beaming cheerfully.

'We can now sleep in peace,' he declared happily. 'And I can do with some sleep. My head, it aches abominably. Ah, for a good herb tea!'

As though in answer to prayer, the flap of the tent was lifted and Hassan appeared, bearing a steaming cup which he offered to Poirot. It proved to be camomile tea, a drink of which he is extremely fond. Having thanked Hassan and refused his offer of another cup for myself, we were left alone once more. I stood at the door of the tent some time after undressing, looking out over the desert.

'A wonderful place,' I said aloud, 'and a wonderful work. I can feel the fascination. This desert life, this probing into the heart of a vanished civilization. Surely, Poirot, you, too, must feel the charm?'

I got no answer, and I turned, a little annoyed. My annoyance quickly changed to concern. Poirot was lying back across the rough couch, his face horribly twisted. Beside him was the empty cup. I rushed to his side, then dashed out and across the camp to Dr Ames's tent.

'Dr Ames!' I cried. 'Come at once.'

'What's the matter?' said the doctor, appearing in pyjamas.

'My friend. He's ill. Dying. The camomile tea. Don't let Hassan leave the camp.'

Like a flash the doctor ran to our tent. Poirot was lying as I left him.

'Extraordinary,' cried Ames. 'Looks like a seizure – or – what did you say about something he drank?' He picked up the empty cup.

'Only I did not drink it!' said a quiet voice.

We turned in amazement. Poirot was sitting up on the bed. He was smiling.

'No,' he said gently. 'I did not drink it. While my good friend Hastings was speaking to the night, I poured it, not down my throat, but into a little bottle. That little bottle will go to the analytical chemist. No,' – as the doctor made a sudden movement – 'as a sensible man, you will understand that violence will not help. During Hastings' absence to fetch you, I have had time to put the bottle in safe keeping. Ah, quick, Hastings, hold him!'

I misunderstood Poirot's anxiety. Eager to save my friend, I flung myself in front of him. But the doctor's swift movement had another purpose. His hand went to his mouth, a smell of bitter almonds filled the air, and he swayed forward and fell.

'Another victim,' said Poirot gravely, 'but the last. Perhaps it is the best way. He has three deaths on his head.'

'Dr Ames?' I cried, amazed. 'But I thought you believed in some occult influence, black magic of some sort?'

'You misunderstood me, Hastings. What I meant was that I believe in the terrific force of superstition. Once get it firmly agreed that a series of deaths are supernatural, and you might almost stab a man in broad daylight, and it would still be put down to the curse, so strongly is the instinct of the supernatural implanted in the human race.

'I suspected from the first that a man was making use of that instinct. The idea came to him, I imagine, with the death of Sir John Willard. A fury of superstition arose at once. As far as I could see, nobody could derive any profit from Sir John's death.

'Mr Bleibner was a different case. He was a man of great wealth. The information I received from New York contained several useful points. To begin with, young Bleibner was reported to have said he had a good friend in Egypt from whom he could borrow. It was understood that he meant his uncle, but it seemed to me that in that case he would have said so. The words suggest some boon companion of his own.

'Another thing, he scraped up enough money to take him to Egypt, his uncle refused to advance him a penny, yet he was able to pay the return passage to New York. Someone must have lent him the money.'

'All that was very thin,' I objected.

'But there was more. Hastings, words spoken as symbols – in other words metaphors – are often taken literally. The opposite can happen too. In this case, words which were meant literally were taken as a metaphor. Young Bleibner wrote plainly enough: "I am a leper", but nobody realized that he shot himself because he believed that he was suffering from the dread disease of leprosy.'

'What?' I exclaimed.

'It was the clever invention of an evil mind. Young Bleibner was suffering from some minor skin trouble; he had lived in the South Sea Islands, where the disease is common enough. Ames was a former friend of his, and a well-known medical man. Bleibner would never dream of doubting his word.

'When I arrived here, my suspicions were divided between Harper and Dr Ames, but I soon realized that only the doctor could have committed and hidden the crimes. Also I learn from Harper that Ames had been friendly with young Bleibner. Doubtless the latter at some time or another had made a will or had insured his life in favour of the doctor. The latter saw his chance to get rich. It was easy for him to inject the elder Mr Bleibner with the deadly germs.

'Then the nephew, overcome with despair at the dread news his friend had given him, shot himself. Mr Bleibner, whatever his intentions, had made no will. His fortune would pass to his nephew and from him to the doctor.'

'And Mr Schneider?'

'We cannot be sure. He knew young Bleibner too, remember, and may have suspected something. Or the doctor may have thought that a further death without motive or purpose would strengthen the belief in a magical cause.

'Also, I will tell you an interesting fact, Hastings. A murderer has always a strong desire to repeat his successful crime. Committing it grows upon him. That is why I feared for young Willard. The figure of Anubis you saw tonight was Hassan dressed up by my orders. I wanted to see if I could frighten the doctor. But it would take more than the supernatural to frighten him. I could see that he was not entirely taken in by my pretences of belief in superstition. The little comedy I played for him did not deceive him. I suspected that he would try to make me the next victim. Ah, but in spite of the damn sea, the terrible heat, and the annoyances of the sand, the brain, the little grey cells still worked!'

Poirot proved to be perfectly right in his reasoning. Young Bleibner, some years ago, in a fit of drunken merriment, had made a jokey will, leaving 'my cigarette case you admire so much and everything else of which I die possessed, which will be principally debts, to my good friend Robert Ames who once saved my life from drowning.'

The case was hushed up as far as possible, and, to this day, people talk of the remarkable series of deaths in connection with the Tomb of Men-her-Ra as clear proof of the revenge of a long-dead king upon those who opened up his tomb – a belief which, as Poirot pointed out to me, is contrary to all Egyptian belief and thought.

About Quick Reads

Quick Reads are brilliant short new books written by bestselling writers. They are perfect for regular readers wanting a fast and satisfying read, but they are also ideal for adults who are discovering reading for pleasure for the first time.

Since Quick Reads was founded in 2006, over 4.5 million copies of more than a hundred titles have been sold or distributed. Quick Reads are available in paperback, in ebook and from your local library.

To find out more about Quick Reads titles, visit

www.readingagency.org.uk/quickreads

Tweet us 🐦 @Quick_Reads #GalaxyQuickReads

Quick Reads is part of The Reading Agency,
a national charity that inspires more people to read more, encourages them to share their enjoyment of reading with others and celebrates the difference that reading makes to all our lives.
www.readingagency.org.uk Tweet us @readingagency

The Reading Agency Ltd · Registered number: 3904882 (England & Wales) Registered charity number: 1085443 (England & Wales) Registered Office: Free Word Centre, 60 Farringdon Road, London, EC1R 3GA The Reading Agency is supported using public funding by Arts Council England.

We would like to thank all our funders:

LOTTERY FUNDED

Quick Reads has something for everyone

Stories to make you laugh

DEAD MAN Talking
RODDY DOYLE

Two women, one man....
RED FOR REVENGE
Fanny Blake

Rules for *Dating a* Romantic Hero
Harriet Evans

JOJO MOYES
Paris for ~~Two~~ One

VERONICA HENRY
A Sea Change

Maeve Binchy
Full House

Stories to make you feel good

Stories to take you to another place

ALEXANDER McCALL SMITH
THE CLEVERNESS OF LADIES
BESTSELLING AUTHOR OF THE NO.1 LADIES' DETECTIVE AGENCY

DOCTOR WHO
THE SILURIAN GIFT
Mike Tucker

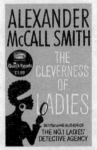

Stories about real life

Stories to take you to another time

Stories to make you turn the pages

For a complete list of titles visit
www.readingagency.org.uk/quickreads

Available in paperback, ebook and from your local library

Discover the pleasure of reading with Galaxy®

Curled up on the sofa,
Sunday morning in pyjamas,
just before bed,
in the bath or
on the way to work?

**Wherever, whenever,
you can escape
with a good book!**

So go on...
indulge yourself with
a good read and the
smooth taste of
Galaxy® chocolate.

Proudly supports

Start a new chapter

Too Good To Be True

Ann Cleeves

When young teacher Anna Blackwell is found dead in her home, the police think her death was suicide or a tragic accident. After all, Stonebridge is a quiet village in the Scottish Borders, where murders just don't happen.

But Detective Inspector Jimmy Perez arrives from far-away Shetland when his ex-wife, Sarah, asks him to look into the case. The gossips are saying that her new husband Tom was having an affair with Anna. Could Tom have been involved with her death? Sarah refuses to believe it.

Anna loved kids. Would she kill herself knowing there was nobody to look after her daughter? She had seemed happier than ever before she died. And to Perez, this suggests not suicide, but murder . . .

Quick
Reads

Start a new chapter

The Anniversary

Edited by Veronica Henry

From family secrets to unlikely romance, from wartime
tragedy to ghostly messages, *The Anniversary* is a wonderful
collection of short stories from some of the best writers
around to celebrate 10 years of Quick Reads.

This collection includes specially written short fiction from
Fanny Blake, Elizabeth Buchan, Rowan Coleman, Jenny
Colgan, Philippa Gregory, Matt Haig, Veronica Henry,
Andy McNab, Richard Madeley and John O'Farrell.

It also includes delicious anniversary
recipes from The Hairy Bikers.

The Anniversary – something for everyone.

Start a new chapter

I Am Malala

An abridged edition

Malala Yousafzai

with Christina Lamb

When the Taliban took control of the Swat Valley,
one girl fought for her right to an education.
On Tuesday 9 October 2012, she almost paid the ultimate
price when she was shot in the head at point-blank range.

Malala Yousafzai's extraordinary journey has taken her from
a remote valley in northern Pakistan to the halls of the United
Nations. She has become a global symbol of peaceful protest
and is the youngest ever winner of the Nobel Peace Prize.

I Am Malala will make you believe in the power of
one person's voice to inspire change in the world.

Available in paperback, ebook and from your local library
Weidenfeld & Nicolson

Quick Reads

Start a new chapter

A Baby at the Beach Café

Lucy Diamond

Evie loves running her beach café in Cornwall but with a baby on the way, she's been told to put her feet up. Let someone else take over? Not likely.

Helen's come to Cornwall to escape the stress of city living. She hopes a seaside life will be the answer to all her dreams. When she sees a job advertised at the café it sounds perfect.

But the two women clash and sparks fly . . . and then events take a dramatic turn. Can the pair of them put aside their differences in a crisis?

Quick Reads

Start a new chapter

On The Rock

Andy McNab

This is the call he is always ready for. They've had word of a planned attack. That's why he's back here, opposite some suit who's trying to tell him what he needs to do. But he knows exactly what's required. Four men. Plain clothes. Eyes peeled. Three targets. Two cases. One car. Gibraltar isn't an ideal location. Too many people. Too many blind alleys. But then again, he's not the terrorist. Who knows what goes through their minds? Well, he will soon. If everything goes to plan.

Available in paperback, ebook and from your local library

Corgi

Quick Reads

Start a new chapter

Pictures Or It Didn't Happen

Sophie Hannah

Would you trust a complete stranger?

After Chloe and her daughter Freya are rescued
from disaster by a man who seems too good to be
true, Chloe decides she must find him to thank him.
But instead of meeting her knight in shining armour,
she comes across a woman called Nadine Caspian
who warns her to stay well away from him. The man
is dangerous, Nadine claims, and a compulsive liar.

Chloe knows that the sensible choice would be
to walk away, but she is too curious. What could
Nadine have meant? And can Chloe find out the truth
without putting herself and her daughter in danger?

Hodder & Stoughton

Quick Reads

Start a new chapter

Hidden

Barbara Taylor Bradford

Drama, heartbreak and new beginnings.
This is a gripping story from a master storyteller.

On the surface, Claire Saunders has it all. She has a rewarding
career in fashion and a talented concert pianist daughter. Her
loving husband is one of the country's most trusted diplomats.

But every now and again, she has to plaster her face in heavy
make-up and wears sunglasses. She thinks she's hidden her
secret from her best friends, but they know her too well.

Can her friends get her out of harm's way and protect
her from a man who is as ruthless as he is charming and
powerful? And along the way, can Claire learn to stop
protecting the wrong people?

Harper

Quick
Reads

Start a new chapter

Rules for Dating
a Romantic Hero

Harriet Evans

Do you believe in happy endings?

Laura Foster used to be a hopeless romantic. She was
obsessed with meeting her own Prince Charming until she
grew up and realised real life doesn't work like that.

Then she met Nick. A romantic hero straight from a fairytale,
with a grand country estate and a family tree to match.

They've been together four years now and Laura can't imagine
ever loving anyone the way she loves Nick.

Now, though, Nick is keeping secrets from Laura.
She's starting to feel she might not be
'good enough' for his family.

Can an ordinary girl like Laura make it work with one of the
most eligible men in the country?

Harper

Why not start a reading group?

If you have enjoyed this book, why not share your next Quick Read with friends, colleagues, or neighbours?

The Reading Agency also runs **Reading Groups for Everyone** which helps you discover and share new books. Find a reading group near you, or register a group you already belong to and get free books and offers from publishers at **readinggroups.org**

A reading group is a great way to get the most out of a book and is easy to arrange. All you need is a group of people, a place to meet and a date and time that works for everyone.

Use the first meeting to decide which book to read first and how the group will operate. Conversation doesn't have to stick rigidly to the book. Here are some suggested themes for discussions:

- How important was the plot?
- What messages are in the book?
- Discuss the characters – were they believable and could you relate to them?
- How important was the setting to the story?
- Are the themes timeless?
- Personal reactions – what did you like or not like about the book?

There is a free toolkit with lots of ideas to help you run a Quick Reads reading group at **www.readingagency.org.uk/quickreads**

Share your experiences of your group on Twitter 🐦 @Quick_Reads #GalaxyQuickReads

Continuing your reading journey

As well as Quick Reads, The Reading Agency runs lots of programmes to help keep you reading.

Reading Ahead invites you to pick six reads and record your reading in a diary in order to get a certificate. If you're thinking about improving your reading or would like to read more, then this is for you. Find out more at **www.readingahead.org.uk**

World Book Night is an annual celebration of reading and books on 23 April, which sees passionate volunteers give out books in their communities to share their love of reading. Find out more at **worldbooknight.org**

Reading together with a child will help them to develop a lifelong love of reading. Our **Chatterbooks** children's reading groups and **Summer Reading Challenge** inspire children to read more and share the books they love. Find out more at **readingagency.org.uk/children**

Find more books for new readers at

- **www.readingahead.org.uk/find-a-read**
- **www.newisland.ie**
- **www.barringtonstoke.co.uk**